Mermaid and Chips

Mary Hoffman

Illustrated by
BERNICE McMULLEN

HEINEMANN · LONDON

For the girls, particularly Rebecca
who wanted to know what happened ne

William Heinemann Ltd, Michelin House,
81 Fulham Road, London, SW3 6RB

LONDON   MELBOURNE   AUCKLAND

First published in 1989
Text © Mary Hoffman 1989
Illustrations © Bernice McMullen 1989
ISBN 0 434 93058 X

Produced by Mandarin Offset
Printed and bound in Hong Kong

A school pack of BANANA BOOKS 31–36 is
available from Heinemann Educational Books
ISBN 0 435 00105 1

Chapter One

BILL BAILEY was a large boy who lived in a small town by the sea. It was a grumpy sort of place, which suited Bill well enough, as he was a grumpy sort of boy. He and his mother lived almost alone, because his father was a sailor who was away from home a lot. At the time of Bill's adventure, they had not heard from his father for about four months and there was no news of when his ship, 'The Neptune', would be back in port. Add to this that Bill's grandad, who used to live with them, had died a few months before and you will see why Bill was not good company. Bill's best friend, Mickey Phipps, was the only one who didn't mind his moods. What Bill and Mickey enjoyed doing was fishing, which they did with a club every weekend during term-time and every day they could manage to spend outdoors during the holidays.

One day, Bill had been standing all afternoon up to his waist in the river Pol and had hardly caught a thing. The other club members were beginning to pack up and head for home. Even Mickey had had enough and said goodbye. Bill was the last one there when he made his final cast.

Immediately, there was a tug on his line
that seemed promising. 'Must be a
trout, at least,' thought Bill and reeled
in as hard as he could. But the fish
resisted him. Bill pulled with every all
ounce of his strength. With a huge plop,
an enormous creature with a fish's tail,
came out of the water and landed on the
bank, knocking Bill over into the river.

When he had staggered, spluttering, to his feet and shaken the water out of his eyes, he simply could not believe what he saw. His fishing-line and hook were caught in the long wet hair of something that looked like a mermaid. Only somehow Bill's brain could not quite accept that message. The creature was a not very young, not very slim woman from the waist up. From the waist down she looked like fish-suppers dinners for a fortnight! While Bill stood dripping and dumbstruck, the mermaid tried to unhook the line from her hair.

'Ye gods and little fishes!' said Bill.

The mermaid sat up abruptly and looked brightly at Bill.

'Come on, ducks,' she said, 'you'd better unhook your catch.'

For the first time in his life, Bill wanted to throw back something he had caught. But he squelched out of the Pol, his waders full of water, and after a bit of a struggle, released his line from the mermaid's hair.

'Ta ducks,' she said comfortably and started combing it with a gold comb, looking at herself in a little mother-of-pearl hand-glass, both of which, Bill realized, she must have been holding when he landed her.

'Er,' said Bill, who had so far said nothing, 'Hadn't you, um, better get back in the river before someone else sees you?'

The mermaid stopped her
hairdressing. 'Get back, dearie?' she
said, puzzled. 'Oh no, that would never
do. You caught me according to all the
rules – you were in the water when I
was on the land – *and* you swore by the
sea gods, so now I have to be your slave
and do whatever you say.'

Bill opened his mouth to speak but the mermaid interrupted.

'Except, of course, for getting back in the river.'

'What do you mean – swore by the sea gods?' asked Bill.

'The gods of the little fishes,' replied the mermaid, and Bill remembered he had used one of his father's favourite expressions of surprise.

Bill didn't know what to do with his catch. He eyed her tail wistfully – it

must contain a lot of fish. But he could hardly take her home to be cooked for supper. 'You can't eat bits of someone who calls you "ducks",' he thought. In the end, he took her home in his bicycle basket, just as if she *had* been his supper. He made her put on his orange plastic raincape which covered her tail pretty well, and, balancing her on the front of his bike, wobbled home to his cottage, with the mermaid giggling all the way.

Bill lowered her to the ground and leant the bike up against the side of the house. He dashed into the kitchen with the few small fishes he'd caught and called out to his mother that he was going down to the village shop for a can of Coke. When he came back out of the house the mermaid was sitting where he'd left her, still wearing the orange cape and smiling cheerfully. Bill had an idea. He went to the shed where they still had his grandad's old wheelchair.

He got it out and put the mermaid in it, wrapping the bottom of the raincape around her tailfin. She was enchanted by the whole thing. Bill then trundled her off to the village shop, because he couldn't think what else to do with her. On the way, she asked him his name and Bill told her. Then it occurred to him to ask:

'Have *you* got a name?'

'Of course, ducks, it's Marina.' But Bill didn't hear her properly.

11

Mickey's mum, who ran the village shop was very interested in Bill's companion.

'Isn't that your poor grandad's old chair?' she asked.

'No it isn't,' said Bill hastily, 'it's my aunty's. That's my aunty, er, Marlene.' The mermaid nodded to Mrs Phipps over her Coke.

'Really?' said Mrs Phipps, suspiciously. 'I never knew your mother had a sister.'

'She hasn't,' said Bill desperately. 'It's my dad's sister. There's something wrong with her legs.'

'Staying with you, is she?' asked Mrs Phipps.

'No! I mean, yes,' said Bill. 'Is Mickey in?'

'He's having his tea,' said Mrs Phipps, nodding to the café next door, where Mickey's dad served fish and chips.

'Can he come up and play after tea?' asked Bill, who could see it was going to be more than a full-time job for one person looking after "Aunty Marlene".

'We'll see,' said Mrs Phipps and Bill hurried out.

When they arrived back at the cottage, Bill's mother had the supper on the table, but Marlene was not ready to let him go in.

'Where am I going to sleep, dearie?' she asked. 'I can't sit out here all night; I'll dry out.'

Bill had a brief vision of stowing Marlene in the bath but the mental picture of his mother finding her there, when she went to clean her teeth, put it out of the question.

'Haven't you got a pond, ducks?' she asked.

'Of course!' said Bill, 'Why didn't I think of that?'

Mickey knocked at the door after tea
with a big bag of greasy chips from the
shop and Bill thought what a useful
friend he was.

'Just going out with Mickey for a bit,
Mum,' he shouted and took his friend
out to the garden.

'Guess what I caught in the Pol after
you'd gone,' said Bill.

'A tiddler,' said Mickey promptly,
'we can have it with our chips.'

'Just for that,' said Bill, 'I won't break it to you gently. Come and meet Marlene.' And he pointed to the pond. Not that you could see the pond, it was all taken up with Marlene's tail. She was fast asleep.

'Cripes!' whispered Mickey, who had gone very pale. 'What's that?'

'It's a mermaid,' said Bill, 'you know, a sort of siren.'

'You mean nee-naw, nee-naw, nee-naw?' said Mickey stupidly.

'No, you wally, the kind who sings and lures sailors onto the rocks.'

'She doesn't *look* like that kind,' said Mickey. 'She's built more like a fire engine. But she's great isn't she, like something out of a film.'

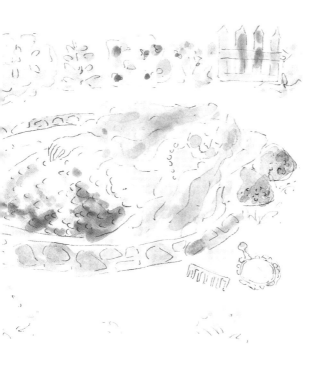

Chapter Two

WHEN BILL WOKE up next morning, he hoped the whole thing had been just a bad dream. His mother was up and off to work early as usual. Bill went to look in the garden. There was Marlene, still occupying all of the goldfish pond. And there was the cat, eyeing her tail with disbelief.

'Morning, dearie,' said Marlene
cheerfully. She was already combing
her hair.

'Morning, er, Marlene,' said Bill. He
looked at her and thought: if she was to
pass as his aunty, he simply *must* find
something for her to wear on her top
half. He found his mother's old
turquoise swimsuit, which she had put
out for jumble. It had glittery stuff in it
and when Bill had cut the bottom off
and given it to Marlene, she seemed to
think it went rather well with her tail.

Mind you, she still didn't look like anyone's aunty, sitting in the wheelchair in her glittery turquoise top, with a bright orange raincape over her knees, or where her knees would have been if she'd had any. The only place that Bill dared to take her was back to the river, where he had arranged to meet Mickey. The other club members looked at her very strangely. But Marlene took to Mickey straightaway. Bill thought it must be the smell of fish that always lingered round his friend. Marlene had a fishy aroma too.

Bill stayed out as late as he dared and suggested more than once that Marlene would be happier back in the river where she came from. But all she would say was: 'No, I must stay with you.'

'How long for?' Bill eventually plucked up courage to ask.

'Forever!' said Marlene comfortingly, giving Mickey a wink.

Bill's troubles were not over when he got home. After he had left Marlene in the fish-pond and gone indoors, his mother had a bone to pick with him.

'What's all this about having an aunty to stay?' she said crossly. She had called in at Mrs Phipps' shop to buy beefburgers on the way home and had heard all about Bill's strange companion of the day before. She had felt a right fool, she said, having to tell Mrs Phipps that Bill's dad didn't have a sister called Marlene, who had something wrong with her legs. Bill didn't know what to say when his mother asked who the woman in the wheelchair had been. His mind went a blank. In the end he said the only thing he could:

'She's a mermaid I caught in the river.'

His mother was furious. 'Bill Bailey!' she shouted, 'You're not too big to have your ears boxed.'

Bill gave up. He took his mother by the hand and out of the kitchen door and round to the back garden. Marlene gave them a cheery wave from the pool and went back to combing her hair. Now it was Mrs Bailey's turn to have nothing to say. She stood like a statue with its mouth open and might have stood in the

same position all night if the smell of burning beefburgers hadn't brought her back to her senses. She and Bill ate their supper in silence. When they had finished, she gave Bill a long look and said, 'I *was* seeing things, wasn't I?'

'Yes,' said Bill, 'you saw a mermaid.'

Bill's mother sighed and went back into the garden, where she was properly introduced to Marlene. Once she had got over her shock, Bill's mother seemed to like her. In fact Bill began to feel quite left out.

'You can't go on sleeping in a fish-pond, my dear,' said his mother, 'not if you're our guest. Wouldn't you be more comfortable in the bath?' And so Marlene moved in with the Baileys. There were still some difficulties of course. When Mrs Bailey served fish fingers, Marlene was very suspicious.

'Where I come from, fish don't have fingers!' she said. But she ate them all the same.

Once Bill caught her trying to pull on his mother's fishnet tights, over her large tail.

'There are some things you have to have legs for,' he told her sternly. But on the whole Marlene and Mrs Bailey got along swimmingly. At last Bill protested.

'You said you'd be my slave and do anything I wanted,' he told Marlene, 'and you haven't so much as conjured up a kipper. You spend all your time chattering to Mum and watching soap operas and sending me off to make cups of tea. What's the use of having a mermaid, I ask you?'

This was a long speech for Bill, as Marlene realised. She straightaway

offered to go fishing with him and, with
her showing him where to cast, Bill
caught so many trout that Mrs Bailey
decided to invite the Phippses in to share
them. That was their first mistake.

It was a Monday, so the Fish and Chip
Café was closed. But Mrs Bailey took
Marlene into the shop part.

'I'd like you to meet my sister-in-law,
Marlene,' she said to Mrs Phipps.

'She's staying with us for a while.
And I wondered if you and Alfie would
like to come and join us for supper
tonight?'

'But, I thought you said . . .'
spluttered Mrs Phipps.

'Oh and bring Mickey too, of course,'
said Mrs Bailey.

'Thank you,' said Mrs Phipps, still
looking very oddly at Marlene.

Mr Phipps was a great joker.

'This is coals to Newcastle all right,'
he said when he saw the fish supper. But
he got on very well with Marlene. In

fact they got on so well that Mickey and Bill started to exchange nervous glances. It would never do for more grown-ups to get involved. Mrs Phipps was a terrible gossip. The trouble was that Mr Phipps had brought some bottles of the local cider, called scrumpy, with him and Marlene soon became rather giggly.

'She's drinking like a fish,' whispered Mickey.

Marlene became careless about her tail and Bill kept having to cover it up with the knitted blanket which he had wrapped round her. She also started to tell some very unlikely stories about her family, having forgotten that she was supposed to be Bill's aunty.

'Ooh, my father's got a horrible temper,' she said. 'He really stirs things up when he's angry.'

'My old man was just the same,' agreed Mr Phipps, opening another bottle.

'Yes,' said Marlene, 'Many's the ship he's wrecked when the mood was on him.'

Mr Phipps gave her a funny look.

'Many's the poor mariner he's sent to Davy Jones's locker . . . ow!' Bill had pinched her tail to shut her up. And in her annoyance, Marlene lashed her

tailfin. Out it flicked from under the rug
and everyone saw it. Bill covered it up
straightaway, but he knew they'd seen.
The party broke up soon afterwards.

31

Chapter Three

ALFIE PHIPPS HAD quite a big queue in
his fish bar the next night. He kept
them all waiting while he tossed the
chips up and down in their wire basket
and told them about Marlene. Mrs
Phipps was battering fish and Mickey
was helping out behind the counter. The
first person in the queue was Hakey
Blake who ran the Aquarium down on
the sea-front.

'So you see,' said Alfie, lowering his voice as he lowered the chips into the hot fat, 'I'm pretty sure she's a mermaid!'

There was a roar of laughter from the people in the queue.

'How many glasses of scrumpy did you say you'd had, Alf?' was the general cry. But Hakey Blake wasn't laughing. He looked thoughtful as he waited for his cod and chips. Mrs Phipps leaned over the vinegar bottles towards him and said,

'I always *knew* there was something fishy about that Marlene!'

Hakey nodded slowly.

'Crumbs,' thought Mickey. 'Dad's blown it now. I'd better warn Bill about Hakey Blake. He'd have Marlene in a tank before you could say pickled onions gherkins.'

But as it happened, Mickey didn't get a chance to warn Bill before Marlene gave him another problem: she wanted to join the local choir. She loved practising her scales in the bath and Mrs Bailey told her she had a lovely voice. So the two ladies set off for choir practice in Zennor church, dragging Bill along to push the wheelchair. While they were waiting for the organist to start, Marlene noticed a wooden carving on a seat in the little church. It was a mermaid.

'Looks a bit like my sister, Oceana,'
she whispered to Bill and dabbed her
eyes with her hankie.

Bill began to hope she was getting
homesick. Or would it be seasick for a
mermaid, he wondered?

Choir practice began and Bill had to
admit that Marlene was good. One of
the men in the choir kept looking at her.
It was Hakey Blake, and afterwards he
bought coffee for Marlene and Mrs
Bailey. Bill didn't like the way things
were going at all.

At last, Bill got Marlene and his
mother away.

'Toodle-oo then,' said Marlene coyly to Hakey Blake, 'see you tomorrow night.'

'What do you mean by saying "see you tomorrow night" to Hakey Blake?' said Bill crossly, as he pushed Marlene home.

'Don't be so rude, Bill,' said his mother. 'Mr Blake has kindly offered to take Marlene out for a meal tomorrow. I call it very nice of him to want to cheer up an invalid like that.'

Bill stopped pushing. 'That's a fine kettle of fish,' he said. 'Marlene is *not* an invalid and Hakey Blake is *not* a kind man. He runs the Aquarium on the front and he's a friend of Alfie Phipps. Don't you think he might just have heard about Marlene's tail and might have a fancy to exhibit a real live mermaid in one of his tanks?'

Marlene and Bill's mother looked at one another, shocked. A big tear rolled down Marlene's cheek.

'I've enjoyed living on the land. But you're right,' she said. 'It's too risky. I didn't mind being caught fair and square by our Bill here, according to the rules, but I'm blowed if I'm going to be trapped and tanked and put on display to make Hakey Blake's fortune.'

Chapter Four

WHEN HAKEY BLAKE came to call for
Marlene the next evening, Bill's mother
met him at the door and said
unfortunately her sister-in-law was not
feeling well enough to come out. But
when she had shut the door, he saw the
tracks of the wheelchair, leading to the
river.

Bill and Mickey were pushing Marlene in the wheelchair back to the River Pol. She was wearing the orange raincape again.

'It's like rewinding a video,' whispered Bill to Mickey. Marlene had explained that Bill had to get back in the water while she was still on the land and then say some special words. They were nearly there when they heard the sound of wheels on the track behind them.

'Quick!' yelled Mickey, 'It's Hakey Blake's van. You run on and get in the river, Bill. I'll push as fast as I can!'

Bill stumbled on ahead in the fading light, wondering if Hakey had a tank in his van and if they were going to save Marlene in time. He ran down the path to the river bank shouting for Mickey to hurry. Mickey was going as fast as he could, but the van was gaining on them,

He gave a sigh of relief as they reached the path, knowing that Hakey Blake couldn't get his van along it. Unfortunately it wasn't too easy for wheelchairs either. Mickey looked back to see if Hakey was pursuing them on foot. Before he could save it, the wheelchair caught on a rut in the path and Marlene sailed out of it in a perfect curve down towards the river.

'Look out!' Mickey shouted.

Marlene landed in Bill's arms just as Hakey Blake pushed past the wheelchair.

'Owzat!' yelled Mickey.

Bill had staggered a bit under Marlene's weight but now managed to pant out:

'Back to the sea, mermaid go free – daughter of foam, I send you back HOME!'

Marlene gave him a salty kiss on the cheek before plopping heavily back into the water. Hakey Blake was dancing up and down on the bank like a madman, seeing his wildest dream of holidaymakers' money swimming downstream. Marlene waved to him cheekily.

'Never mind Mr Blake – there are plenty more fish in the sea!'

When she was in the middle of the stream, far out on her way to sea, she

called to Bill and Mickey. 'Go down to the harbour tomorrow and you'll see me again.'

Next morning Bill ran to the harbour. He shouted for joy as he saw his father's ship ''The Neptune'' sail into port. It was a modern ship but it had acquired an old fashioned figurehead of a mermaid. Bill blinked and looked again and the figurehead winked and waved and dived off the ship into the water. His mermaid had done something for him after all!